The Modern Magi

Other Loyola Press books
by Carol Lynn Pearson

A Christmas Thief

A Stranger for Christmas

CAROL LYNN PEARSON

*The*

## Modern Magi

*a christmas novel*

LOYOLAPRESS.
CHICAGO

# LOYOLAPRESS.

3441 N. ASHLAND AVENUE
CHICAGO, ILLINOIS 60657
(800) 621-1008
WWW.LOYOLABOOKS.ORG

*Cover design by Eva Vincze*
*Interior design by Eva Vincze*

**Library of Congress Cataloging-in-Publication Data**
Pearson, Carol Lynn.
    The modern Magi : a Christmas novel / Carol Lynn Pearson.
        p.   cm.
    ISBN 0-8294-1763-X
 1. Gifts—Fiction.   I. Title.
    PS3566.E227M63   2003
    813'.54—dc21

                                          2003001622


03  04  05  06  07  08  09  10 Bang 10 9 8 7 6 5 4 3 2 1

# Chapter One

*Annabelle Perkins* was on the mailing list of Tour the World Travel Agency, located downtown. She had asked to have her name taken off most of the other lists she had been on—Time/Life record collections, Fireside Theatre, even *Guideposts,* and the little catalogs that offered address stickers and key-chain flashlights. She was a serious saver and didn't want to be tempted to spend money on frills. But she kept her name on the mailing list of Tour the World because that's what she was saving up for: a trip to the Holy Land.

There's not much to tell about Annabelle, not much to know, really. She was a very average woman, fifty-seven years old, who grew up and went to school in Cincinnati. Her only brother had died in Vietnam. Her father had owned a restaurant, and her mother had taught school. But in the last five years, first her father, then her mother had passed away. Since Annabelle had never married or had children, after her parents died, she was very much alone.

There were two things Annabelle inherited that she counted as her most prized possessions. The first was a glove that her father claimed once belonged to Theodore Roosevelt. The story was that President Roosevelt had been in Cincinnati and had eaten at her father's restaurant. When he left, there was a glove under his chair, and her father had decided to keep the glove and send President Roosevelt a contribution of twenty dollars for his next campaign fund, reasoning that twenty dollars would buy *two* pairs of gloves.

"Yes sir," he would say to guests at the restaurant about the glove that was framed with a picture of the president, "that glove was on the hand of Teddy Roosevelt himself, who, by the way, said our black-bean soup was the best he'd ever tasted. Could we start you with a bowl of that for your lunch?"

The other prized possession was even more prized, for it belonged to Jesus. It was a small bronze lamb, lying down with its sweet little nose resting on its right foot and its eyes looking up at you mournfully.

"Do you know why this little lamb is so sad?" Annabelle remembered her mother asking when she was little. It became a favorite question that would begin a favorite story: "Because all of his friends went to Bethlehem to see the baby Jesus, but he got lost and ended up in the hill country and missed everything. *But . . . ,*"— and here her mother always paused for effect and snuggled Annabelle down into the blankets—"*someday* this little lamb is going to go to Bethlehem, did you know that? And this little lamb is going to be a gift for the baby Jesus. Have I told you about the baby Jesus?"

Of course she had, dozens of times, but Annabelle always looked at her with wide eyes and said, "Tell me."

And her mother would tell Annabelle once again about the baby Jesus, whether it was Christmastime or not. But, of course, she told it more often and more fervently just before Christmas—told of the little baby come to teach the world how to love, how to forgive, how to become like he was, like God. And every time she told the story she stroked the little bronze lamb and said, "This little lamb is going to go to Bethlehem one day, for this little lamb is going to be our gift to the Christ child, just as the wise men gave gold and frankincense and myrrh. This little lamb—you think it's bronze, don't you? But it's really gold, as gold as the gold of the Magi. And because Jesus sees how things really are instead of just how they look, he will know this is gold and very valuable. Just as he looks at us and knows how really wonderful we are even though we look ordinary. And when we give this gift to Jesus, we're going to hear him say, 'Thank you.' You can hear Jesus talk, you know. If you listen hard, you can hear him. Sometimes I hear Jesus talking in my mind, telling me things."

So that was how Annabelle knew that the lamb belonged to Jesus. And because of the way her mother's voice sounded whenever she talked about Jesus, Annabelle knew that her mother loved him very much, and even more, she knew that he loved them very much and that the gifts he had given them could never be repaid.

Annabelle especially liked to hear her mother talk about how Jesus saw people the way they really were, instead of how they looked. She knew that when Jesus looked at her, he saw a perfect person, not someone who had a heart problem, someone who had had rheumatic fever as a child, which led to endo-carditis that had affected her mitral valves and left her with a systolic murmur, which meant that she had to be more careful than most people and not overdo it. Jesus didn't care about any of that. He knew that the real Annabelle and her heart were perfect.

She never quite knew how much was pretend about her mother saying that they would take the lamb to Jesus one day. But after her mother died, Annabelle was going through the family things, and her hands were suddenly holding the little bronze-but-gold lamb. She heard herself saying out loud, "This little lamb *is* going to go to Bethlehem, and *I* am going to take it there. It will be my gift to the Christ child. From me and from my mother, who loved him so much and never got to go."

And then Annabelle sat down, breathless and frightened, and drank some lemonade. She was not accustomed to doing remarkable things. In the sixth grade, she had gotten the Citizen of the Month award. That was special. In high school, she had sung in the choir and had gotten a certificate of excellence, but everyone in the choir got one—so it wasn't special. And one time, she had marched in an antiwar demonstration. Well, she was just crossing the street when they came along, and she got swept up in it; and thinking about her brother in Vietnam, she walked with them for three blocks and felt herself very brave and remarkable. But—going out of the country to the Holy Land? Actually going to Bethlehem? She found the little bronze lamb, and he looked at her with his mournful eyes. . . .

Annabelle breathed deeply, got up, and opened the telephone directory.

# Chapter Two

When Annabelle walked into the travel agency after taking the bus downtown, Mr. Olson smiled at her just as if she were a rich lady come to buy another ticket for a cruise to the Caribbean, not as if she were a very poor lady who had never even been to Florida, which was the truth.

"And what can I help you with today?" he beamed, his round face rising like the sun from his desk, where he'd been arranging travel brochures. "Please—sit down."

Annabelle sat hesitantly and began. "I'd like to find out about—the Holy Land. I want to go there."

"Ah!" Mr. Olson beamed even brighter. "The Holy Land." He reached toward the rack and brought back a fistful of colorful brochures. "Here we are!" His voice made her feel as though their plane had just landed near Bethlehem. "Here we are!"

"How much is it?" asked Annabelle, wanting to get the worst part over first.

"Hmmm. Well, let's see. That depends. We have a nice three-week package in Israel and Egypt, the Holy Land Complete, for . . . hmmm . . . thirty-five hundred."

"Oh!"

"That includes airfare, of course, lodging, and two meals a day."

"I don't need Egypt."

"Something shorter then?"

"Yes."

"Well—the Holy Land Adventure—two weeks, twenty-eight hundred. Five days in Jerusalem—"

"I don't need Jerusalem."

Mr. Olson looked at her curiously. "I beg your pardon?"

"I just want Bethlehem. Do you have something that only includes Bethlehem?"

"Hmmm. I don't believe there is an airport in Bethlehem. You'll have to fly into Tel Aviv. Well, here's a nice option for those who are pressed for time."

What a nice man, Annabelle thought. Did he really think she was pressed for time?

"Christmas Adventure in the Holy Land!"

Oh, that would be lovely, thought Annabelle. To go at Christmastime!

"One week . . . Sea of Galilee and Golan area . . . Judean Wilderness . . . Bethlehem."

"How much?"

"Two thousand dollars."

"Airfare, lodging, and two meals a day?"

"Of course."

Annabelle was about to tell him that she didn't need two meals a day, that one would do if she kept bread and apples or dates in her purse, but something extravagant seized her and she said, "Well, that sounds just fine!"

"That will require a two-hundred-dollar deposit," said Mr. Olson. "But we won't need that for a few months. It's only March. July will be fine for the deposit, or June to be sure."

Annabelle pulled a roll of bills from her purse. "No, I want to make the deposit today."

And she counted out ten twenty-dollar bills onto his desk.

Outside as Annabelle walked to the bus stop, one hand held her coat closed against the wind, and the other held her purse full of brochures. She felt very powerful. She had done something remarkable. Surely the people on the sidewalk could see it as she walked. She was not an ordinary fifty-seven-year-old woman hurrying to catch the 5:46 bus home. She was one of the Magi on a fabulous journey. Stars and moons were watching, and angels were preparing to sing. She was going to take a gift to the baby Jesus!

At home at her kitchen table with raspberry tea steaming in front of her, Annabelle opened a brochure, tacked it up on the wall with straight pins, sharpened a pencil, and went to work. Two thousand dollars. Minus two hundred. Eighteen hundred. Eight months to get eighteen hundred. Nearly two hundred and twenty-five dollars per month.

She could do it. Waitressing three days a week at the restaurant her father had sold gave her enough to live on, but not much to save. But they would let her add another day, even though the doctor had told her to remember that her heart condition was not getting any better and that she should not overdo it. But she was Frank's daughter, and they would let her add another day if she asked for it. They all knew that the family money had been used up by her mother's lingering illness. They would be happy to help her.

The next month, she had three hundred and forty dollars in cash, which she put in a brand-new savings account. She kept the passbook in her stocking drawer, along with the different brochures that had begun to appear in the mail. Every month a new one arrived, full of palm trees and bullfights and listings of all the tour offers. And every month she would sit down and scan the new brochure carefully, as if she were looking for her own name on a program.

There it was! Christmas Adventure in the Holy Land.

And every month the money would go into her savings account. Her special money for Jesus.

# Chapter Three

*At the end of October* the total had reached eighteen hundred dollars. She hadn't dared tell anyone about her plans, thinking superstitiously that if she told, something might happen and she wouldn't be able to go after all. But that was silly. Especially now that she had the money in hand. Today, for the first time, she would dare share her precious secret. But whom should she tell? . . . Someone at the restaurant? Today was Friday. Of course! Almost every Friday, Mr. and Mrs. Somersby came in and always ordered the day's special. For two or three years she had been waiting on them, and they had exchanged little pieces of family news. She knew all about their daughter in college and their son who just got married. And they had sent flowers when her mother died and had even attended the funeral service. They would be thrilled for her.

"Well, there you are!" Annabelle said as she brought over a tray of water glasses. "It's almost quitting time, and I was getting worried about you two."

But they weren't two, they were three. Today an attractive young girl in her early twenties sat between them, her reddish hair pulled up in a curly ponytail.

"This is our daughter, Marianne. Marianne, this is Annabelle, who gives me one day out of the kitchen every week, and am I ever grateful." Mrs. Somersby smiled warmly.

"Hi." Marianne smiled her mother's smile.

"Well! The college girl! I know all about you!"

"Oh, really?"

Annabelle raised one hand as if giving a proclamation. "Three-point-seven grade point. Majoring in elementary education. Wrote a paper on creating safer hallways that the teacher read to the entire class."

Marianne blushed and put her head down. "Mo-om!" She said the word like all children whose privacy has been invaded, but there was still a bit of a smile.

Annabelle slid three glasses of water and three napkin-wrapped sets of silverware off her tray and onto their table. "I am *so proud* of you,

Marianne! We need good teachers like you. Two semesters left—or is it three?"

"Two." Marianne spread the napkin on her lap and stared at it.

"And you're here for a visit? How nice."

There was a moment of silence.

"Well, actually," said Mrs. Somersby gently, like you do when you're trying to make something bad sound like something good, "Marianne is going to be staying with us for a while. She's looking for work."

"I'm quitting school."

"Quitting?" Annabelle looked at Marianne as if she were the teacher and Marianne a kindergartner who had torn up the best picture book. *"Why?"* Then she caught herself. "I'm sorry. This is none of my business. I just—please forgive me." Annabelle quickly handed out three menus.

This time it was Mr. Somersby who spoke.

"That's all right, Annabelle. We know that you care. Well, I don't mind telling you that this is due to *my* problem. Three months ago I lost my job."

"Oh! I didn't know."

"And things are not looking good in my field. Others have been out of work for two years or more. So . . . " He shrugged.

Marianne added, "My student loan did come through, but it doesn't quite cover all the expenses, even tuition. And a minimum-wage job doesn't—" Marianne broke off and took a sip of her water.

"I see. I—I understand. Well, I'm sorry."

"It'll be all right. I'll work for a year or so, help with things around here, save up," Marianne reassured Annabelle.

"I think we're ready to order now," said Mrs. Somersby brightly. "The fish special, I think. . . . "

As Annabelle brought their order, steaming from the kitchen, and placed a bowl of minestrone soup in front of the sweet girl with the reddish ponytail, her heart hurt.

It was then that she heard the voice. *"You can give me the gift now."*

Annabelle did not look around. She knew the voice was not behind her or to the side of her. Her hand froze in midair.

*"You can give me the gift now."*

Later that night, at home alone with her raspberry tea and her toast, Annabelle heard the voice for the third time. She already knew who it was and what it meant: It's what her mother was talking about when she said Jesus spoke to her in her mind. And it certainly did sound like the voice of Jesus, though she would have been hard-pressed to describe what Jesus' voice ought to sound like. But then again, it also sounded like her mother's voice. And her own voice.

Give him the gift now?

What if she did it—did what she thought this voice was telling her to do? What if she took the money she had saved up for her trip to the Holy Land—all eighteen hundred dollars of it—and gave it to that sweet girl so she wouldn't have to drop out of school? She'd have to do it in secret, of course.

The very thought was thrilling and terribly, terribly sad. Was she actually thinking about giving up the "Christmas Adventure in the Holy Land"? Was she really considering *not* taking the gift to Bethlehem, *not* giving Jesus the little bronze-but-gold lamb?

"You can give me the gift now."

Annabelle finished the last of her tea and then got out the old typewriter so that nobody could recognize her handwriting.

*Dear Marianne,*

*This is a gift from me to you and to Jesus. I don't want you to drop out of school and neither does he. There are too many little children who need to have a good teacher like you. Please stay in school and teach the children to be good.*

*A Friend*

# Chapter Four

*The following day,* after Annabelle dropped the letter with the money order into the mail slot at the post office, she found herself walking. Just walking. She didn't want to go home. Not yet.

Dried leaves made a scratching sound on the pavement as a breeze blew through. Annabelle pulled up the collar of her coat, but she didn't feel cold. She felt warm, very warm. The scene in her mind was so real. Tomorrow the Somersbys would bring in their mail, Mrs. Somersby, probably.

"Well, here's a letter for Marianne. Marianne!"

Marianne would enter the room and take the letter and a puzzled look would cross her face. "Hmmm. No return address. What in the world?" She would open it. She would read it.

And then—

Annabelle's eyes blurred and the leaves became one carpet, not hundreds of individual leaves. Just one.

Well, she was only two blocks from Tour the World Travel Agency. Maybe she ought to go in and explain that she wouldn't be going on the Christmas Adventure in the Holy Land after all. Silly, she thought. As if they would miss her. As if the whole staff would stop work and say, "Why, where is Annabelle Perkins? She's supposed to be on the Christmas Adventure in the Holy Land tour and she's not here. Quick, somebody—go find Annabelle!"

Well, Mr.— what was his name? Mr. Olson. He *had* been very nice, and she didn't like to leave people hanging.

Just as Annabelle crossed the street to the travel agency, she saw red and gold Christmas decorations in a store window, and her heart felt that it would burst. Christmas! Christmas Adventure . . .

Mr. Olson was very understanding. Annabelle explained that some things had come up, some rather important business things, and going this year was just not convenient.

"The deposit? Well, I really ought to check with the boss. No. No, I think I can safely say that your deposit will be good for next year. I think I can safely say that."

Next year. Annabelle lifted up the calendar in her kitchen. *Next year.* The words sounded so terribly unfriendly. She had been saying five months, four months, three months, and now she had to say next year. Well, the only way around it was through it, that's what her mother had always said. Next year.

She lifted up the calendar as if to reassure herself that next year was really coming. There it was, right after December. Next year.

# Chapter Five

*On the Fourth of July* Annabelle decided to treat herself to the whole works: parade, picnic at the church, and fireworks in the park. She went with the minister's family, with whom she often spent holidays since her parents were gone.

Sitting there at the picnic table, indulging—as she *never* did—in a second piece of fried chicken, Annabelle was in such a celebratory mood that she told the minister and his wife all about the trip she was planning.

Here it was only July, and she had already earned the money again. In fact, she had more than enough. She had saved up twenty-four hundred dollars. Business had been good at the restaurant, tips had been good, and she had gotten back more on her tax return than she had expected, which she didn't understand but was not about to argue with.

Well, she didn't tell the minister and his wife *everything.* Not about the little lamb as a gift for Jesus. They might think that was silly, and giving the gift was too important to her to have anyone thinking it was silly.

"Well, Annabelle," said the minister admiringly. "The Holy Land! That's been a dream of mine, as well. You'll have to give us a full report."

Later that afternoon, Annabelle was tearing off the front page of the *Daily News* the minister had finished reading, so she could use it as padding around the bottles of pickles and ketchup that were going back into the picnic basket, when a photograph caught her eye.

Oh, my. That looks like . . . A man with curly brown hair and a very square jaw stared up at her. Tom? She read the caption. It *was!* There on the front page of the *Daily News* was a photograph of Tom. A woman was with him. And three children: a little boy who looked to be about eight and two teenage girls.

Annabelle sat down on the bench and leaned against the table. She hadn't thought about Tom for a long time. Not *really* thought about him. He was always there in the background of her mind, like the way the sound of plates and laughter in the kitchen were always there when she was in the restaurant. But it had been a long time since she had taken his memory out and turned it over and over, examining it the way she used to.

She had been in love with Tom in college. In fact, he was the only man she'd ever really loved. They'd had an English class together and dated for three months. And they'd even kissed, and it had been wonderful. He stopped calling soon after she told him about her heart condition, and she always figured that was why.

Tom loved to ski and bicycle and climb hills. She'd guessed that he couldn't see himself with a wife who couldn't keep up with him, and for a while she'd hated him for that. Of course, she never knew for sure what he'd been thinking, and maybe it wasn't her heart condition at all.

She glanced at the picture. The woman was

nice enough looking, but not what you would call beautiful. The children *were* beautiful, really beautiful. Is that how theirs would have looked if . . . ?

Why in the world was Tom in the paper? She read the headline: LOCAL FAMILY SEEKS HELP FOR KIDNEY TRANSPLANT. Quickly she scanned the story. Tom's wife—her name was Jennifer—was failing rapidly with a diseased kidney.

What a shame. Those beautiful children.

She continued scanning the article. The only hope was a transplant. The insurance would pay for only part of the cost. A donor had to be found within three months, which the doctors thought was possible, and fifty thousand dollars had to be raised, which was the hard part. The chances for a successful operation were high with a prognosis of a completely normal life.

Oh, my.

Annabelle quickly put down the paper and walked over to where the children were playing volleyball. She had to get her mind on something else before . . .

*"You can give me the gift now."* The voice was soft but very, very clear.

No. No, this was a mistake. Her mind was just making this up, playing tricks to tease her. If she watched the children playing ball, it would pass. Soon it would be time for the fireworks, and her mind would be back to normal.

There. The minister's son Mark slapped the ball over the net hard and down to the ground. The boy's mother cheered the loudest. "Way to go, Mark!" And he lit up like a Christmas tree.

Christmas. Christmas Adventure in . . .

Boys need their mothers to cheer for them.

No. Absolutely not. She didn't owe him anything. In fact, he had hurt her terribly. *No!*

Annabelle was glad to go to the fireworks. Anything to keep her mind filled with sound. She leaned up against a tree and watched the little comets soar into the sky and then explode into breathtaking showers of colors. Again and again—the bullet sounds of firecrackers, the booms of the bright show in the sky, the "ahhh's" of the people with upturned faces.

*"You can give me the gift now."*

No!

Annabelle walked back and forth on her kitchen linoleum with a teacup in her hand, barely managing to keep the hot liquid from spilling over the edges.

This was not fair. It was asking too much. No!

She went to her desk and pulled out the brochure, the special one that had the pictures she had looked at over and over again. The brochure barely hung together where it creased. "Christmas Adventure in the Holy Land." *That's* where she wanted to go! *That's* where she wanted to give him the gift! She wanted to do it remarkably!

*"You can give me the gift now."* It was the only sound in the little kitchen, and there was no way she could ignore it.

Annabelle sank into the chair. "Do I have to?"

*"No."*

Tears pushed their way out from between Annabelle's closed eyelids and fell onto her hands. In her mind were thoughts, clear as photographs: a mother holding a baby wrapped in swaddling clothes; a mother holding a baby that looked a little like Tom; a mother watching her baby crucified; three children watching their mother growing weaker in a hospital bed, not the color she ought to be. And then the pictures of the mothers and the children became one, and the face was a gentle and beautiful face.

And Annabelle had the strangest feeling—as though she were about to tiptoe into the most wonderful room and leave the most wonderful present under the most wonderful tree, and she couldn't wait to hide and watch the face of the someone who would open it.

She felt—so powerful. She was not used to feeling so powerful. And warm. And she was smiling.

Annabelle stood up and got out the old typewriter.

*Dear Tom and Jennifer,*

*I wish I had fifty thousand dollars, but this is all I have. I am going to pray that many others will send some, too, and I know that you will have the amount that you need. I saw your picture in the paper. You are a beautiful family. And I hope you have a very happy Christmas.*

*A Friend*

# Chapter Six

*A few days later,* after spending some time adding and subtracting columns of numbers at her little wooden desk in the kitchen, Annabelle gave up. There was no way in the world, between July and November, that she could save the money again. And her doctor was insisting that she cut back at work. Next year. There it was again. *Next year.*

Mr. Olson understood. Again. Annabelle explained that some things had come up, some different things, and it just didn't look like she could make it this year. Mr. Olson nodded his head.

"But next year—oh, I'm certain. I will make absolutely certain that next year I am on the Christmas Adventure in the Holy Land tour. Now, about the deposit—"

It was not easy the next year saving up the money, not as easy as she thought it was going to be. She had longer to do it, but then she had cut back at work, and not only because her doctor insisted. She was feeling it herself, feeling her energy giving out, often feeling that she really ought to go and sit down. As soon as she saved up the money, she would probably take the early retirement they had offered her at the restaurant and then volunteer to spend two days a week at the hospital nearby. If there was something she could do sitting down, of course.

This time she didn't deposit her savings in the bank as she had before. She kept it in the closet hidden inside a very, very old rain boot. Of course this was not a wise thing to do, and Annabelle knew that, but she wanted to keep the money close to her. She wanted to be able to count it out every week when she added to it, putting the fifties in a pile and the twenties in a pile and the tens in a pile, and watching those piles grow thicker and thicker.

It was November fifteenth when she finally had the money—twenty-two hundred dollars. The price of the tour had gone up two hundred dollars, and she didn't know for sure whether

her deposit was still good. Mr. Olson had said "probably," but she couldn't count on that.

She put the money in a large envelope inside another envelope and placed it inside her blouse and buttoned a sweater on top. Of course she would not risk putting the money in a handbag and going downtown like that. Nobody had ever grabbed her purse and ran, but she read such terrible stories in the newspaper all the time.

It was a beautiful, nippy fall day when she stepped outside her apartment for the walk to the bus stop. Autumn had been unusually long and pleasant. The rain last night had washed the morning clean, and now the air was clear and crisp and had adventure in it. Autumn always felt like adventure to Annabelle, like the starting of a new year of school when you never knew what to expect.

Well, *this* year Annabelle did know what to expect. And it would be the greatest adventure she had ever had.

What happened next happened very, very quickly, and that night as Annabelle sat going over it in her mind, it seemed unreal, like a dream.

As she turned the corner at Hazel on the way to Forty-seventh Street, she smelled smoke. A few seconds later she heard the sirens. Then she was hurrying with more and more people down the sidewalk and across Forty-fifth Street. She could see the flames then, leaping high and orange against a smoke gray sky.

The crowd pushed her forward.

"Would you look at that?" a man whistled low. "It's done for."

"Never knew a house could go so fast."

"Just like tinder wood. I got tiles on my roof. Ought to be illegal to have anything but tiles on your roof."

Annabelle stood behind a boy on a bicycle and had a clear view. Firemen were just bringing an old man out of the front door. His drawn face was smeared with soot, and they were all coughing. A woman with a small child beside her burst into tears as she saw them emerge. Breaking loose from the arms of neighbors who had been restraining her from going back into the building, she ran to the old man.

A moment later a car screeched to a halt and a man ran through the crowd, crying out, "Let me through! Let me through!" He saw the little group—the woman, the child, and the old man—and embraced them sobbing, "Thank God! Oh, thank God!"

At that moment the roof crashed down with a mighty clap, sending up a shower of sparks that made the crowd gasp and draw back. The firemen worked steadily with their hoses, but everyone else in the crowd seemed frozen to the earth, watching in wide-eyed horror as a house disappeared, as all the familiar things that made life comfortable for four people went up in smoke. Everyone watched unmoving.

Except one woman.

Annabelle lifted her face a little, then nodded as if someone had spoken to her.

And then, smiling as if it were the only thing to do on this November morning, indeed as if it were exactly what she had gotten out of bed and dressed herself to do, Annabelle calmly walked from the crowd up to the little family huddled together in the front yard, reached inside her sweater and blouse, and brought out a bulging envelope, warm from its place near her heart. She pressed it into the man's hands, gently touched the cheek of the weeping woman, and whispered, "Merry Christmas," then turned and walked back into the crowd.

# Chapter Seven

*That evening in her kitchen,* Annabelle played over and over the events of the day and examined with surprise her feelings about them. Of course this meant that her plans for the Christmas Adventure in the Holy Land were gone—and something within her was very certain that they were gone, not just one more time, but forever. Because of her heart condition, she could not take another year of waiting tables. She had been reassigned to making salads, so she couldn't even count on the tips anymore. She felt weak when she walked to the post office and back, and that was only six blocks.

But—and this is what surprised her—she didn't feel that something wonderful she had so looked forward to was suddenly taken from her. She felt instead that something wonderful she had so looked forward to had *already happened!* She felt—and of course she must be crazy—but she felt as though she had just returned from her Christmas Adventure, and it had been absolutely everything she had dreamed it would be. Strange. Very, very strange.

On the morning of the fire, she had continued down to Tour the World Travel Agency. Mr. Olson had understood. Again. And he nodded his head in a very sympathetic way as she said that she had decided not to go to the Holy Land after all, that she thought she might just go to Philadelphia instead. That wasn't really a lie. An uncle and aunt in Philadelphia had been inviting her for years, and she thought that maybe she ought to take them up on it.

So now, as Annabelle sat at her kitchen table with her raspberry tea and the sweet little lamb in front of her, she stroked the metal nose and said, "I'm sorry. But we will do something lovely at Christmas, I promise."

You can imagine Annabelle's confusion, then, when her phone rang just one week later and she heard a voice say, "Miss Perkins?"

"Yes?"

"This is Mr. Olson of Tour the World Travel Agency."

"Yes?"

"I wanted to remind you that we'll need your passport number to give to the airlines by Friday."

"I beg your pardon?"

"I'm so glad you changed your mind."

"Passport? Do I need a passport for Philadelphia?"

"For Israel, Miss Perkins. For the Holy Land. For the Christmas Adventure in the Holy Land."

"But I'm not going on the Christmas Adventure in the Holy Land."

"But you're on the list. My records show that your fee has been paid in full."

"There's some mistake, Mr. Olson."

"Well, let me look at these papers again. Hmmm. There you are. Annabelle Perkins. Amount paid, twenty-two hundred dollars. Amount due, zero."

"But I didn't—I never—"

"Of course, it's entirely up to you, Miss Perkins. All I can tell you is that the Christmas Adventure in the Holy Land is expecting you, and we need your passport number by Friday. You do have a passport number?"

"Oh . . . oh, yes!" Annabelle dropped the phone and ran to the desk drawer. She grabbed the passport she had applied for two years before and fished the colorful brochure from her wastepaper basket. Then she sat down and pressed a hand to her heart. All this excitement! "My number, my passport number is . . ."

And then she went for a walk. She could not sit still, could not stay inside her drab four walls when a miracle was happening. Who? Who in the world would have done such a thing? Money does not just show up in people's travel accounts. Mr. Olson said there was no way to tell who had done it and simply refused to discuss the matter any further.

Oh, my. Someone, *someone* had taken twenty-two hundred dollars—well maybe just two thousand, depending on what they had worked out about the deposit—and paid it to Tour the World so Annabelle Perkins could take her trip to the Holy Land!

She shook her head. This is not possible. People just don't do things like that.

And then she heard the voice, that sweet, solemn voice with just a bit of a laugh in it this time. *"Well, Annabelle, do you think you're the only one I ever talk to?"*

# Chapter Eight

*Annabelle packed her suitcase* very, very carefully. And as she did she felt like one of the Magi. Theirs had been a long, hard journey to get to the Holy Land, but it had taken *her* three years—no, it had taken her a whole lifetime!

How should she pack the lamb? There was tissue paper in the top cabinet in the kitchen. And then she could put it inside a wool stocking for extra protection. She smiled and shook her head. A Christmas stocking. A gift for the blessed baby. She searched her bottom drawer and found a thick red stocking. But her mind trailed off again in the direction she had been pulled ever since the miracle had happened.

*Who* had done this wonderful thing? She had spent a month now looking suspiciously at everyone. So few people even knew. The minister and his wife? They didn't have that kind of money. Jacob at the restaurant? The Somersbys? Her doctor? A secretary at Tour the World Travel Agency? Mr. Olson, of all people?

She had even looked suspiciously at strangers and made up the wildest scenarios. That man in the rich-looking suit on the bus, carrying the heavy briefcase—maybe he was a multimillionaire. Maybe he had seen her months ago and had said to himself, that woman deserves something glorious. Maybe he had hired a private detective who had learned of her Christmas Adventure in the Holy Land.

She had laughed at the thought. And then had gone on to make up another outlandish scenario about the woman with the odd smile and the birthmark on her cheek who was driving the bus, pretending to be *just* a bus driver.

Or, wait! Maybe someone on the tour— someone she had never even met—had done it. Maybe some couple from Brooklyn or San Francisco had called Tour the World and said, "Is everything set for the tour? Everybody ready to go? Is there anyone who—you know—needs a little extra help?"

Well, they *could* have done that. Oh, it was delicious! She would never, never look at anyone the same way again.

Annabelle pulled a kitchen chair over to the cabinet and stood on it, one hand holding the little lamb tightly, the other hand reaching up to where the gift wrap and tissue paper were carefully layered under the silver tray that her mother used to get out of the cupboard once a month for her club meetings. Seeing the silver tray always reminded Annabelle of the excitement of something happening, something bright and colorful between long stretches of gray. Oh, she wished her mother could see her now. *This* was excitement! *This* was the most exciting thing Annabelle had ever known or ever dreamed of. Sometimes she had to remind herself to breathe, it was that exciting.

She reached up and pulled a sheet of paper from under the tray. And then a strange sensation, a little squeezing pain went down the length of her left arm and into her chest. For a moment, she thought she was falling, falling off the chair and onto the floor.

But then she realized she wasn't falling at all. She was rising, rising up above the chair, up above the cabinet. Why was she higher than the silver tray? Who was that person lying on the blue-and-white-checkered linoleum, clutching a small bronze lamb exactly like the one in her . . . ?

Her hand was empty!

An odd buzzing sound filled the room. The ceiling dissolved as if it were frost on a warm morning, and she saw a long, dark opening, like a tunnel.

Then a voice. "Oh, Annabelle, Annabelle! He *loved* your gifts!"

Who was that woman rushing toward her? Why—could it be—? "Mother!"

"He *loved* your gifts!"

"My gifts?"

Annabelle glanced down at the little lamb. That was the gift she wanted to give him, and she dived to grasp it in her hand. But her hand went through it. And then an even stranger thing happened. The little bronze-but-gold lamb began to glow, to shine radiantly and brilliantly. Then it burst into a thousand pieces and cascaded around her, brighter than all the fireworks of a lifetime. One piece flashed an image of a college girl running to class with an armload of books. Another piece flashed an image of a family on Christmas Day helping a mother recovering from surgery make her way into the family room. Another flashed an image of a couple gratefully buying clothing with a fifty-dollar bill fished from a large envelope. Other pieces were words, smiles, prayers, touches. They went on and on, showering her with light and warmth.

Then she heard another voice. *"Oh, I did love your gifts, Annabelle. Thank you!"*

As she turned in the direction of the sound, she would have caught her breath if she'd been breathing. So beautiful! How could anyone be so beautiful? An angelic personage radiating a brilliant light! She wanted to bathe in that radiance as though she were thawing from a long, long winter. That wonderful warmth would surely heal every cell of her being.

The little speech Annabelle had prepared to say when she got to the Church of the Nativity in Bethlehem was gone—vanished from her mind, and somehow she knew her trip to Bethlehem was gone, too.

"Oh," she said, simply. "I thought—I wanted so to bring you something—in the Holy Land."

*"I'm not there anymore, Annabelle. I'm wherever you need me to be."* He smiled. *"And now I must tell you something. I have watched you come*

*and go in your own home, your own town, and, Annabelle, the ground that you have walked has become as holy a land as there is on this earth."*

Warm arms reached out, and Annabelle moved into them.

When Mr. Olson of Tour the World Travel Agency learned what had happened, he sank back in his chair, closed his eyes, clicked his tongue, and shook his head. What a shame. She was a sweet, strange woman, and it was a crying shame.

But Annabelle didn't think it was a shame. Looking back on it, she felt that her surprise Christmas adventure was better—oh, far better—than her best dreams.

Carol Lynn Pearson has been a professional writer, speaker, and performer for many years. Her poems have been widely reprinted in diverse publications, such as Ann Landers' column, *Chicken Soup for the Soul,* and college literary textbooks. Her poems are now also available in a compilation, *Picture Window.*

Her autobiography, *Goodbye, I Love You,* tells the story of her marriage to a homosexual man, their divorce and ongoing friendship, and her caring for him as he died of AIDS. This story made her a guest on such programs as *The Oprah Winfrey Show* and *Good Morning America.* She has also been featured in *People Magazine.*

Ms. Pearson has written numerous educational motion pictures, including the well-known

*Cipher in the Snow,* as well as many plays and musicals, two commissioned by Robert Redford's Sundance Theater.

A major contribution of Ms. Pearson has been writing and performing a one-woman play, *Mother Wove the Morning,* in which she plays sixteen women throughout history in search of the feminine divine. The play was performed over three hundred times internationally and is now available on a videotape that earned an award from *Booklist* as "one of the top twenty-five videos of the year."

A series of seven inspirational books, Fables for Our Times, began with *The Lesson,* a look at life as a series of story problems, and includes *Will You Still Be My Daughter?* and *Girlfriend, You Are the Best!*

Her recent book *Consider the Butterfly: Transforming Your Life Through Meaningful Coincidence* includes forty-four of her personal stories that show how the phenomenon of synchronicity can bless our lives daily.

Ms. Pearson has an M.A. in theater, is the mother of four grown children, and lives in Walnut Creek, California. You can visit her at *www.carollynnpearson.com.*